MY BOOK OF

Giants

CONTENTS

Reprinted by permission of
William Jay Smith
Illustrated by Peter Richardson

Marshall Cavendish

THE FARMER, TOMT AND THE TROLL

-WANTED-

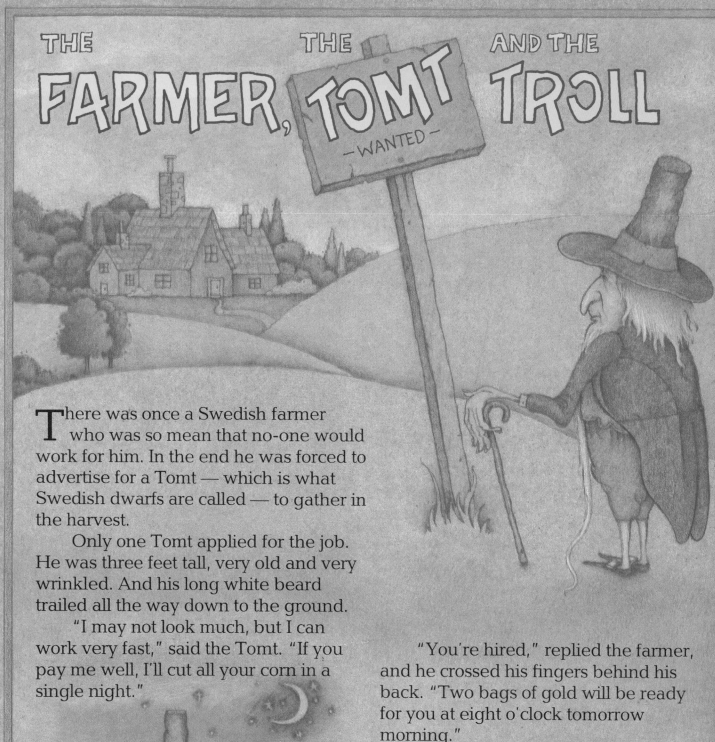

There was once a Swedish farmer who was so mean that no-one would work for him. In the end he was forced to advertise for a Tomt — which is what Swedish dwarfs are called — to gather in the harvest.

Only one Tomt applied for the job. He was three feet tall, very old and very wrinkled. And his long white beard trailed all the way down to the ground.

"I may not look much, but I can work very fast," said the Tomt. "If you pay me well, I'll cut all your corn in a single night."

"You're hired," replied the farmer, and he crossed his fingers behind his back. "Two bags of gold will be ready for you at eight o'clock tomorrow morning."

Before the Tomt set off for work, he sang a song:

"I shall scythe and I shall reap
While the farmer's fast asleep.
In the morning, draw my pay,
And hop, skip, jump, I'll be away."

All night long the little Tomt toiled and by seven o'clock in the morning the entire wheat crop had been harvested and neatly stacked in the barn.

"Finished at last," said the Tomt, and at eight o'clock he knocked on the farmer's door.

He knocked once, he knocked twice, he knocked three times — but there was no reply.

He bellowed through the letter-box. He threw pebbles at the shutters. At last the farmer poked his head out of a window and shouted, "What's all the fuss about?"

"I want my pay," said the Tomt.

"Well, you can't have it now — come back this time next year and I'll see what I can do." And he slammed the window shut.

The poor little Tomt was so furious at being cheated that he went off to a nearby hill to plan his revenge.

It was a very odd shaped hill and when the Tomt reached the top, he found he was standing on the end of a huge nose.

"Good heavens," he said to himself. "This isn't a hill at all, it's a Troll! And I have been trampling all over him with my dusty shoes!"

"I don't mind," said the Troll. "It's lonely up here and I like a little conversation now and then."

So the Tomt told the Troll his sad story, and the Troll was absolutely furious. "Fancy cheating a poor little Tomt like you."

Then the Troll had an idea. "Let's visit the farmer together. I'm sure he'll pay up when he sees you've got a big brother like me." So they marched off to the farm.

The farmer was eating his dinner when he heard a loud knock at the door. "Who's there?" he growled.

The Tomt shouted through the letter-box, "Will you please pay me my wages. Get the money and be prompt. Do not make me wait for ages. It's bad luck to cheat a Tomt."

"Go away," growled the farmer. "I won't pay." Then he looked out of the window and saw a gigantic Troll armed with a wooden club standing outside.

"If you don't pay, you'll lose your hay," said the Troll, and with a mighty puff he blew all the farmer's haystacks into the pond. Then he leaned on the roof until it creaked and said very quietly, "Pay or I'll crack your chimney stack."

But frightened as he was, the farmer was too mean to hand over any money, so the Troll lifted the roof and peered inside.

The farmer was sitting on the kitchen floor, hugging his bags of gold. With a trembling hand, the farmer held up one bag, "Will this do?" he asked.

"Not enough," said the Tomt.

"Two bags?"

"That's right," said the Tomt, grabbing his wages.

"And one for me," said the Troll, stuffing another bag of gold into his pocket.

Then the Tomt climbed on to the Troll's huge shoulders and they marched away, singing a victory song:

"Tomts and Trolls must stand together,
If they are to get their way.
Now we're off to spend the money
On a seaside holiday."

JACK AND THE BEANSTALK

Once upon a time, there was a poor widow who had an only son called Jack. Jack was not much help to his mother. He did not earn any money, and the two of them were very, very poor. Then, one day, their one cow finally became too old to give any more milk.

"It's no use," said Jack's mother. "We'll just have to sell her."

So Jack led the cow off towards the market, promising to get the best possible price for her. But the journey was long and boring, and Jack passed the time dreaming about what he would buy if he were rich.

On his way he met a funny little man with a big head and a tiny body, who offered to buy the cow.

"Give her to me and I promise you'll be rich to the end of your days," he said, holding out a small drawstring bag.

Jack could hardly believe his ears. But when he opened the bag instead of gold coins, he found it contained only five shrivelled beans!

"Those beans are magic," said the little man. "Plant them and they'll grow right up to the sky!" And before Jack could say anything he vanished — and so did the cow!

Jack ran back home, wondering what would happen when he planted his magic beans.

"You were quick," said his mother, when Jack arrived home. "How much did you get for the cow?"

"I struck a wonderful bargain," he said. "Look at this!"

When his mother looked inside the bag she was furious. "Beans! Beans? You stupid, lazy good-for-nothing boy! Do you want us to starve?"

Jack tried to tell her that the beans were magic, but she would not listen. She flung them out through the window, then beat poor Jack and packed him off to bed without any supper.

The next morning, a very hungry Jack woke early. At least he *thought* it must be early because the room was so dark. But when he turned over he saw

a huge green plant outside the window with giant leaves pushing through the shutters. "So! The beans were magic ones after all!"

Quick as a flash, Jack clambered out through the window and on to the enormous beanstalk. Stopping only to wave goodbye to his astonished mother standing below him, Jack began to scale the giant plant.

He climbed and he climbed. He even climbed right through the clouds.

Then, suddenly, a long wide road stretched out in front of him. Jack walked for hours, and just as he was thinking of turning back he saw a great castle. Tired and hungry, Jack knocked on the towering door. It was opened by a huge woman. She looked down at him and Jack looked up at her.

"Please could you give me something to eat?" he asked. "I'm very hungry."

"Be off with you. My husband will be back soon and he eats little boys like you for dinner."

But Jack pleaded with her, and in the end she let him in and gave him some bread and cheese. He had almost finished, when he heard great footsteps thudding along the passage.

"Oh dear!" cried the giant's wife. "It's my husband. Quick, hide in the oven."

Jack just had time to scramble into the oven when the kitchen door flew open and a great big bald-headed giant burst in. He sniffed the air and roared:

Fee, fi, fo, fum,
I smell the blood of an Englishman.
Be he alive or be he dead,
I'll grind his bones to make my bread.

"No, no, no, dear," said his wife calmly. "You're mistaken. Now sit down and eat your meal."

When the giant had finished his colossal dinner he took out a vast box full of bags and sat down to count his money. Peeping out from the oven, Jack caught his breath at the sight of so much gold!

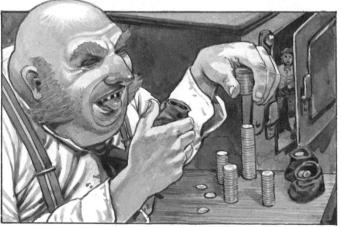

Soon, the giant's head began to nod and he dropped off to sleep. Jack leaped out, threw one of the bags over his shoulder and sprinted out of the castle. He ran all the way along the road, then dropped the bag down on to the ground far below and clambered through the greenery of the beanstalk to his house.

For months Jack and his mother lived very well, but soon only a few gold coins remained. And one day, when his mother went to wake him, she found he had gone back up the beanstalk to find more gold.

"Oh, it's you again, is it?" said the giant's wife when she opened the castle door. "The last time you were here my husband lost a bag of gold."

"Really?" replied Jack. "How strange! Perhaps I can help you look for it. I'm small enough to fit into all the nooks and crannies you giants can't reach."

So the foolish giant's wife let Jack into the house again, and she even gave him some bread and cheese.

Jack was still pretending to look for the lost gold when he heard the footsteps of the giant coming home. He just had time to dive into the oven when the door burst open and the giant sniffed the air and roared:

Fee, fi, fo, fum,
I smell the blood of an Englishman.
Be he alive or be he dead,
I'll grind his bones to make my bread!

"No, no, no, my dear. I think you're mistaken. There's no-one here. Now sit down and eat your meal."

The giant held a little white hen in his hand, and when he had finished his meal he put it on the table. "Hen, hen, one two three, lay a golden egg for me!" and the hen laid the strangest egg Jack

had ever seen. It was made of solid gold! The giant chuckled greedily and then nodded off to sleep, clutching the golden egg.

Jack sneaked out of the oven, clamped his hand round the hen's neck and sprinted out of the castle, along the road and back down the beanstalk.

With the magic hen strutting around their yard, Jack and his mother were rich at last, and they said they would be happy for ever. But one morning, when his mother went to wake him, Jack had gone!

This time when Jack climbed the beanstalk and reached the castle door, he did not dare to knock, but crept inside while the giant's wife was fetching in the washing. And instead of hiding in the oven, he hid in the washtub.

11

Soon, he heard the footsteps of the giant in the passage and the door burst open. The giant sniffed the air and roared:

Fee, fi, fo, fum,
I smell the blood of an Englishman.
Be he alive or be he dead,
I'll grind his bones to make my bread!

"Surely not," said his wife. "But if you *can* smell that thieving boy who stole your bag of gold and your hen, he'll be hiding in the oven for sure."

The giant pounced on the oven door — but of course Jack was not inside.

"You really shouldn't upset yourself like that," said the giant's wife. "Now, why don't you get out your little harp?"

So the giant did. "Play," he said. And the little harp began to play sweet music.

The giant sighed happily, his wife sighed happily — and they both dozed off to sleep in their chairs.

Quick as a flash Jack jumped out of the washtub, snatched up the harp and ran out of the door. Then, suddenly, the harp cried out, "Master! Master! I'm being stolen!"

The giant woke up with a start. "What! Hey you! Stop! Bring me my axe!" Jack sprinted down the long road, the giant gaining with every stride, his massive feet pounding and his huge voice roaring for Jack's blood.

Jack reached the beanstalk just a few paces ahead of the giant, threw himself into its green mass, and slithered down the trunk. The bellowing giant tumbled after him, crashing through the branches, swinging his axe wildly.

"Fetch my axe!" Jack shouted to his mother as he reached the ground. Working furiously, Jack chopped away at the stem of the beanstalk as the giant emerged through the clouds. Then, with a creak and a groan, the beanstalk began to fall. It fell right through the roof, through the house — CRASH! — on to the ground. And the giant fell headlong into the vegetable patch with a mighty roar, and broke his neck!

Then Jack showed his mother the harp and asked it to play sweet music.

With the hen that laid the golden eggs, and the harp that made such lovely music, Jack and his mother lived happily for the rest of their days.

STOLEN THUNDER

Thor, God of Thunder, woke up in Valhalla. It was a beautiful morning, and Thor was full of life. "Today I shall hammer on the mountains until the whole world shakes to the sound of my thunder! The noise will echo down the fjords and shatter icebergs in the Northern Sea." And he sprang out of bed. "Now where did I put that hammer?"

But Thor's magic hammer — the thunderbolt — was nowhere to be seen. He looked under his bed. He lifted up his clothes — the thunder clouds — which were scattered around his bedroom. He emptied his cavernous cupboards. He opened his door and his voice boomed through the great hall of Valhalla, "Where's my hammer?"

In the end his friend Odin had to come and help him look — and realised that Thor's hammer had been *stolen*.

"But who would dare to steal from Valhalla?" roared Odin, King of the Gods.

"Who but the Giants?" said Loki, God of Mischief.

So Odin comforted Thor, and tried to calm him down, while Loki borrowed the flying cloak from Queen Freya, wife of Odin. And Loki flew down to the Realm of Giants.

"Yes, I know where Thor's hammer is. It's buried, fifty fathoms deep under the ground. I know, because I put it there myself. And I won't give it back until Queen Freya comes down here to be my bride!" He laughed, opening a mouth as deep, dark and dirty as a cave, with teeth like broken rocks. "And when you send her, tell her to bring her flying cloak and her golden necklace. Haw! Haw!"

Loki kept his temper, and smiled evenly. Then he flew back to Valhalla, and repeated the message to Odin, King of the Gods. "Din will not give back Thor's hammer unless we give him your wife, Freya, as a bride."

Odin's eyes blazed with anger — grey and wild like the sea, then white and swirling like the sky, then hot and red as fire. "My wife as his bride!"

The first person he met there was the giant Din.

"Do you know where Thor's hammer is?" Loki asked.

Din, the biggest and the dirtiest of the giants, grinned from ear to ear. He scratched himself, and a cloud of dust rose up and made him sneeze. But he wiped his nose on his sleeve and went on grinning.

"Ah," said Loki. "But I have a plan."

Two bright shapes flew down through the clouds, and across a dark landscape to the door of Din the giant. Loki had brought a bride for Din, wrapped in the magic cloak and adorned with the gorgeous golden jewellery of Freya, Queen of the Gods.

Then Din prepared a sumptuous wedding feast. The tables groaned under the weight of food and the barrels of red wine. All the giants were there (though none of them had washed specially) and their scrawny dog slunk under the tables, scrounging any food that was dropped. Din watched with delight as his bride sat down to eat.

First she ate a side of roast beef, then a shoulder of pork, then a broiled swan — then she picked her teeth with a bladebone. And she drank so much wine that Din had to send out for more.

"She's got quite an appetite, this Freya of yours," said Din. "How does she keep her figure?"

"That's easily explained," Loki replied smoothly. "She hasn't eaten all day because she's so thrilled at the thought of marrying you."

Din blushed. "Well, well. So she wants me that much, does she?"

"You've never seen a woman more excited! I almost think she must have been secretly in love with you for years and years ."

Din jumped to his feet. "For that she deserves a kiss! Come here, my little sugar-mouse!"

"Why is she looking at me like that?" he whispered to Loki.

"Can't you tell?" answered Loki. "She couldn't sleep a wink last night, for the thought of you. And now she sees you, she can't take her eyes off you!"

"Oh," said Din nervously. "Good."

As the banquet came to an end, Loki coughed politely and remarked, "I don't like to mention it on so happy an occasion, but do you think we could have Thor's hammer back now? That was the agreement."

And Din clapped Loki on the back and roared, "Of course, Loki, old friend. A deal's a deal — I get the woman, you

But his bride looked at Din with eyes as blue and wild as the sea, which then turned as white and swirling as the sky, then as hot and red as fire.

Din gulped and stepped back, rather alarmed.

get the hammer! Servants! Bring me Thor's thunderbolt right away."

The doors opened wide and a steely grey hammer was carried in. Three giants staggered and grunted under its weight. Then Din laid the hammer down in front of Loki.

"How I wish Odin was here!" Din gloated, edging towards his bride. "I'd give anything to see his face when Freya sits on my lap and starts kissing me . . ."

"You have your wish!" bellowed the bride. And there, throwing off his disguise, stood Odin, King of the Gods! He snatched up the hammer. "And here — you shall have your kisses!" He swung the massive hammer in the air, and smashed it down

three times on Din's fat head. Then Odin swept through the hall, felling giants on every side. Within seconds, all lay sprawling on the ground — and the dog gobbled up the rest of the banquet.

Odin and Loki flew back to Valhalla, where Freya and Thor were waiting.

"Thank heavens," she said. "I don't know why you're wearing that dress, dear, but I'm glad to see you've got Thor's hammer back. He's been impossible since it was stolen."

With the hammer back in his hands, Thor was happy again. He whooped with joy! And then he beat on the mountain tops until the whole world shook, and the thunder echoed down the fjords and shattered icebergs in the Northern Sea.

MASTER of the LAKE

In a small hut in a far-off land, there lived an old couple who were very poor. They had no sheep, nor horses, nor goats — not even a hive of bees to give them honey. When they died, they left their son Avram nothing but a few strands of flax scattered on the floor.

Avram took these down to the lake, dipped them into the water and set about plaiting the wet strands into a rope. While he was working, the fearsome Master of the Lake rose from its watery depths and stood before him. Though he was very frightened, Avram tried not to show it.

"What are you doing here?" the green, bearded giant cried.

"I'm plaiting a rope. When it's ready, I'm going to hang your lake from the clouds!"

This strange, brave reply struck fear into the Master. "No, no, boy!" he cried. "Don't touch my lake, I beg you! I'll grant you any wish you like, but leave my waters in peace."

Avram thought hard. What should he ask of the giant? The lake was famous locally for the beautiful wild horses that watered there so, he made up his mind. "Give me your finest horse, and I'll not touch your lake."

"Oh no! Those horses are my fame and my strength!" cried the Master. "I can't grant *that* wish."

"As you please," replied Avram. "Then I shall have to hang your lake."

The Master of the Lake was silent. Perhaps he suspected a trick. "Well, boy," he said at last, "if you are strong enough to hang my lake, you won't refuse a test of strength between us first. We'll race round the lake. If you overtake me, I'll grant your wish."

"Agreed!" said Avram. "There's just one thing. I have a younger brother. He's sleeping in the bushes over there. If you can beat him first, *then* I'll race you round the lake myself."

The giant went into the bushes at the edge of the lake — and out scampered a frightened hare. At once the Master of the Lake gave chase. But of course, he could not catch the hare, no matter how fast he ran.

"I'll beat you yet!" he shouted to Avram in a rage. "Let's fight!"

Avram agreed. "Oh, but first you must beat my old grandfather. If you can knock him off his feet, I'll leave the lake to you. There he is, resting in that hollow. He's er, a heavy sleeper, so you'll have to give him a crack over the head to wake him."

Off went the Master to the hollow where a big brown bear was dozing. He gave the bear a crack over the head with a big stick — which did not please the bear. Leaping up, it seized the Master of the Lake in its strong arms and threw him crashing to the ground.

Limping back to Avram, the giant cried, "How strong your grandfather is! I've no strength left to fight you. But give me one last chance.

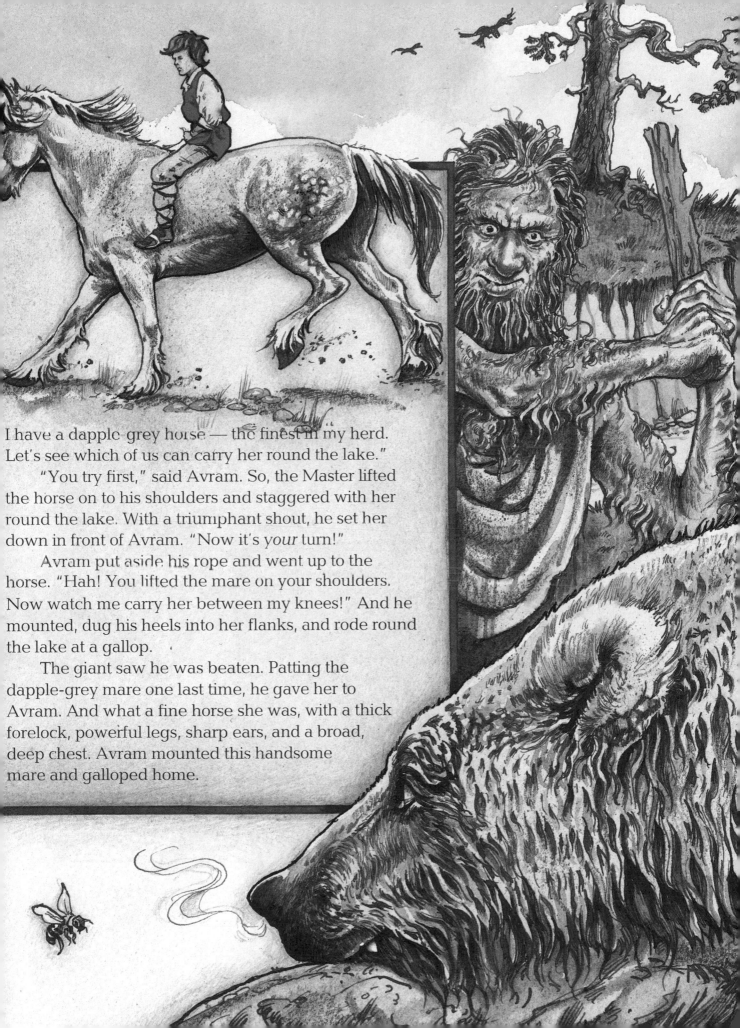

I have a dapple-grey horse — the finest in my herd.
Let's see which of us can carry her round the lake."

"You try first," said Avram. So, the Master lifted
the horse on to his shoulders and staggered with her
round the lake. With a triumphant shout, he set her
down in front of Avram. "Now it's *your* turn!"

Avram put aside his rope and went up to the
horse. "Hah! You lifted the mare on your shoulders.
Now watch me carry her between my knees!" And he
mounted, dug his heels into her flanks, and rode round
the lake at a gallop.

The giant saw he was beaten. Patting the
dapple-grey mare one last time, he gave her to
Avram. And what a fine horse she was, with a thick
forelock, powerful legs, sharp ears, and a broad,
deep chest. Avram mounted this handsome
mare and galloped home.

BiG GUMBO!

Great big gawky Gumbo Cole
Couldn't stop growing to save his soul.
Gave up eating, gave up drink,
Sat in the closet, hoped to shrink;
But he grew and grew till he burst the door,
His head went through to the upper floor,
His feet reached down to the cellar door.
He grew still more till the house came down
And Gumbo Cole stepped out on the town
And smashed it in like an old ant-hill!
Never stopped growing, never will,
Ten times as tall as a telephone pole,
Too big for his breeches — Gumbo Cole!